DATE DUE

DEBRA DI BLASI

DROUGHT

—— & ——

SAY WHAT YOU LIKE

A
NEW
DIRECTIONS
BOOK

Book design by Sylvia Frezzolini
Manufactured in the United States of America
New Directions Books are printed on acid-free paper.
First published as a New Directions Paperbook Original in 1997
Published simultaneously in Canada by Penguin Books Canada Limited

Library of Congress Cataloging-in-Publication Data

Di Blasi , Debra , 1957–
Drought and say what you like / Debra Di Blasi
p.   cm.
ISBN 0–8112–1332–3 (alk. paper)
I. Title.
PS3554.I1735D7   1997
813'.54—dc20   96–24621
CIP

New Directions Books are published for James Laughlin
by New Directions Publishing Corporation,
80 Eighth Avenue, New York 10011

DROUGHT

PART ONE: JUNE

House

The house sits one hundred and twenty yards from a bleached gravel road, beneath two misplaced elms that offer little shade except in the evening when a dry wind rises from the valley and shade is no longer necessary. It is a white house, small and anemic beneath a white sun. The paint on the clapboard peels away from the grayed wood and falls like confetti among the stunted shrubs and dying flowers.

On the side facing east, a mound of dirty sand partially blocks the wide dark entrance of a basement half-finished then abandoned to decay. Weather inhabits this yawn. In winter it moves deeper and upward into the house, so that when the man and woman shout or make love or battle nightmares, their breath is visible.

But it's June now. It's summer. There's just heat, inside and out.

Woman

Her name is Willa. Her father was illiterate. He named her after that particular species of tree with long thin branches like a woman's hair: *Willow.*

But he said, "Willa."

Weeping Willa.

Except she never cries. Not anymore and not for years. When she was nine, her two big cousins raped her and then burned a tiny heart onto the white skin over her breastbone with a hot pocketknife. The burn blistered, then scabbed over, then became a scar. It was then she decided: *Crying heals nothing.*

Unlike her father, she is educated. The only one in the family to finish college. Unfortunately, she studied art. Yet, less than a continuing poverty, she fears her family history of ignorant violence, which she suspects may be genetic and therefore inescapable.

Drowning in air

To the east of the dirty sand pile a bed of chalky limestone juts outward, forming the low cliffs which overlook a valley. The road into this valley is a south road—south of the cliffs, south of the house. It's made of dirt. When the rains come, it turns soft and the pickup tires plow deep ruts into it. But it hasn't rained for nearly a month so the road is hard. And dry: when the pickup heads down into the valley, clouds of yellow dust rise behind it and hang for a moment in the hot still air.

In the valley there's an old wide deep pond stocked with bass and crappie and blue gill. Beyond the pond are hills covered with timber. Among the timber is a creek that feeds the pond in spring when the snow melts and the rains come and the water overflows the creek bank and rushes down the hillside.

The creek is almost dry now. The pond's water level steadily declines; its perimeter shrinks. Fish leap above the surface all day long as if fleeing the thickening crowds below, as if trying to drown themselves in air.

Self-portrait

She bends over a wooden table which rests against her left thigh and picks up a misshapen tube of oil paint. A brown strand of hair falls from her chignon onto her white neck where tiny beads of sweat gather, slide away, then gather again.

Every window in the house is open. There are no screens. Insects fly in and out, day and night.

As she unscrews the cap from the tube, a flesh fly lands on her left elbow. She blows on it twice in short audible breaths. It rises, circles her head, then lands on her right shoulder. Again she blows on it and again it rises and circles. It settles on her forehead, just above her left eyebrow, a fraction of an inch from a large bead of sweat that's about to slide away.

She pushes her lower lip outward and blows. The sweat slides. The fly bites.

Sarcophagidae

"Flesh flies lay their eggs on decaying organic matter such as dead animals, rotting fish, or manure. The amount of eggs is vast. Newly-hatched larvae of just a few flies can make a corpse wriggle and squirm as if it were alive again."

—Bill Buford's Bug Book
for Beginners, Volume 4

For two years she painted nothing but delicate watercolors of insects: illustrations for an entomologist who writes bug books for children. Now when she paints a self-portrait, she sees antennae instead of hair, labrum and labium instead of lips. And rising behind her head, sprouting from her shoulders: *wings!*

Light

With two fingers she squeezes the tube until a small white spot of paint appears on the glass palette. Her shoulders rise as she inhales through her nose, then slowly fall. She lifts her head. With her left hand she reaches toward the table, picks up a brush, and carefully lowers it onto the small white spot on the glass. When her hand rises again, it trembles almost imperceptibly.

A bright flash of light enters through the window behind her, striking the rivers of sweat, the edge of the comb protruding from her chignon, the golden hairs of her left forearm, the white tip of the brush raised in a false salute.

Her eyes are gray and cold. Like granite. They shift to the left, away from the brush, as her head turns toward the window and into the light.

Landscape

From this window there is only the struggling green of trees, the yellow grass, the bright purple of thistle heads. And in the distance, beneath the pale sky growing paler: the low valley and pond lying prone at the feet of the opposite hills. I feel surrounded here, suffocated.

It's as if each day God reneges and takes back a wedge of air.

Heron

The oar moves in slow deliberate strokes through the water, first on the left, then on the right. Within the ripples gathering on the surface is the distorted reflection of an arm, its muscles contracting with each downward swing of the oar.

At the far end of the pond where the bank shifts from clay to buckbush, a diseased elm stands dying against the colorless sky. A single branch—skeletal, a dry gray bone—sways from the sudden weight of a great blue heron. The bird cocks its head to the side, listening, then forces a mournful call into the silence it discovers.

The oar stops. The muscles relax.

Man

The man's first name is Kale, the surname of his maternal grandfather. It's an old name, at one time significant in this poor rural county. Synonymous with *land* and therefore *wealth*. Now everyone surnamed Kale is in the cemetery. They're dead. No one thinks of them, except the groundskeeper who arranges his tending schedule according to family plots and so considers the Kales (along with the Millers and the Talberts) only on Thursdays.

Kale does not even think of the Kales. Until someone suggests his name was derived from a variety of cabbage. A comment which he sometimes, though not always, feels obliged to dispute.

Rain

He looks up at the sun and closes his eyes. He drops a hand over the side of the canoe and folds his palm around the warm water. He removes his glasses and lifts the wet palm and rubs it over his face and thinks of rain:

How it would green the drying fields.

How it would put meat back on the cattle, fill their shriveled udders.

How it would be nice to wake early some morning to the sound of water rushing from the eaves, a mist coming through the window and onto the bed, the woman wrapping her legs around his waist, her nipples growing hard, palatable, in the cool damp air. . .

Pond

When he puts his glasses back on, his eyes move out over the shuddering pond. They climb onto the hard clay bank, sift through the stubble and weeds of the valley, ascend the white wall of cliffs, peer through the big open window that looks out over the cliffs and yellowing valley and quiet pond.

This pond: where the man is just now dipping his oar into the water, the canoe turning in such a way that it catches the sun and sends a single ray of light out over the landscape. A single ray which does not stop until it strikes the white tip of a brush poised in mid-air.

Name

She turns into the light. To no one—not even herself—she says, "Kale."

PART TWO: JULY

Woman, man

She leans away from the canvas and glances in the direction of the kitchen: "What are you looking for?"

He says, "Beer."

She wipes the paintbrush on a rag, drops it into a jar of turpentine, then sets the jar on the floor. She lifts the hem of her skirt and wipes the sweat from her breastbone where a tiny pink scar of a heart remains.

"Willa, what happened to all the beer?"

"You drank it last night."

"I bought two six-packs yesterday."

"Are you standing with the refrigerator open?"

"Two goddamn six-packs."

"Please close the refrigerator."

She stares at the canvas, then stands and pats the loose strands of hair into place absently, ineffectively. She is young—twenty-five—broad-shouldered and broad-hipped. When she moves to the window to stare out at the cliffs and valley and pond and hills, her body shuts out enough light to make the room noticeably darker.

There, against the late afternoon sun, she lets her forehead fall against the hot pane and releases a sound which resembles that of a dying animal.

Radio

. . .Another day of record-breaking temperatures and still no rain. The overnight low was eighty-seven degrees. Today's high was a cool one hundred and eight. Holy mackerel! One hundred and eight! Better find yourself a nice big swimming pool and set up residence, folks, 'cause forecasters are predicting at least another week of unseasonably hot weather. . .

Resemblance

The kitchen is nearly dark. She walks in. He's bent over in front of the refrigerator, hands on knees.

"There is no beer, Kale."

"I can see that."

"Then shut the goddamn fridge."

"It feels good."

She goes to the sink and picks up a dirty glass and holds it up in the light. She turns on the faucet and sets the glass beneath the water and watches the water fill the glass, then overflow. Gnats rise and veer. Her hands rest on the edge of the sink like two lumps of clay.

He stands straight, closes the refrigerator: "Want to go with me to buy some beer?"

"No."

"How about some wine, then?"

"No."

"Scotch?"

She looks at him. In the fading light, she thinks he resembles her father.

Drunk and poor

Three years ago she told him, "You're nothing like my dad."

He said, "That's a damn weird thing to say at a time like this."

"Why?"

"Because."

"Because?"

"We just screwed and now you're talking about your father."

"It's got nothing to do with sex."

"What, then?"

"I don't want to get stuck with somebody like my dad. No education. No ambition. Drunk and poor."

"Don't worry. That's not me."

"If it was, I'd leave you."

"It's not."

"Or if I couldn't leave you, I'd kill you."

"It's not me."

It's hot

"How about some wine, then?"

"No."

"Scotch?"

Her eyes blink once. "How about some sobriety, Kale?"

He moves behind her and wraps his arms around her waist and presses his face against the back of her neck.

"Willa's in a bad mood. Did Willa have a shitty day?"

She turns off the water and empties the hot glass into the sink. She peers at the dark hole of a drain and sees that particles of food have accumulated there. She becomes conscious of Kale's body heat, the sweat developing along her spine. She squirms. "It's hot."

His arms tighten. "Is it?"

He rubs the stubble of his chin against her neck until her skin becomes pink, then red.

"Yes, *hot*."

She breaks his hold by turning sharply to her right and goes to the refrigerator and opens it and takes out a large jug of water. She pours the water into her glass and drinks it down. She looks at the empty glass, then at the jug. Very slowly, without expression, she tilts the jug and pours the cold water over her bare feet. It pools on the linoleum and runs in a wide river toward the center of the room.

He looks at the water on the floor, then at her face which is blank.

"Jesus Christ, Willa."

She shrugs her shoulders, puts the empty jug back into the refrigerator and repeats, "It's hot."

It's a small house

There are three main rooms: a living room, a bedroom and a kitchen. Each room occupies a quarter of the house: southeast, northeast and northwest, respectively. In the southwest quarter is a bathroom and a small open space into which the front door leads. The space is cluttered with coats and boots and shoes and tools and boxes and a shovel and a spade and an ax.

Each quarter of the house meets at a single point, dead center. There are three doors positioned exactly sixteen inches from this point, one for each main room, so that it's possible to walk from the living room to the bedroom to the kitchen to the open space and back into the living room while creating a 360° line: a perfect circle.

Spinning in circles

When she was four she asked her mother why dogs spin in circles before they lie down. Her mother said, "It's how they pray, honey. How they keep the devil out of their dreams."

Shortly thereafter she found her mother crawling around and around on the bed, panting and drooling, whispering and hissing, "Get him out of my dreams, Lord, out of my wetness!" She was taken to the state mental hospital where she died ten months later. Doctors claimed she suffered from "violent, painful, erotic dreams." Claimed she slept fitfully, then stopped sleeping altogether, then stopped speaking, stopped eating.

She never stopped spinning in circles.

Handwriting

The house is sparsely furnished. In the kitchen there's a small round Formica table and two chairs. In the bedroom is an old bureau, a bentwood rocker held together with baling twine, and a box spring and mattress which lie directly on the floor. In the living room is a small green couch and an oak rocker near the stone fireplace whose mantle is stacked to the ceiling with books. There's an easel in front of the big open window. Near the easel is a stool and a wooden table covered with misshapen tubes of paint. Directly to the right of this, in the southeast corner of this room, is an oversized oak desk made level by means of a piece of cardboard folded in quarters and slipped beneath the front leg. The top of the desk is clean except for three beer cans, an ink pen and a spiral notebook with pale green pages. On the page lying open, tiny uneven handwriting begins on the top line and continues one-third down the page where it ends suddenly, without punctuation, without the sentence having been completed, without

Buzzard

He walks through the dusty pasture with one arm outstretched, one finger pointing systematically to each cow. His boots are spattered with fresh manure. With each step he takes, swarms of flies rise from the dark green piles. He reaches the center of the herd and lowers his arm and looks toward the horizon. He sighs. Very slowly he begins counting again.

At the north end of the pasture is a narrow grove of cottonwood trees growing along the bank of the creek and up the other side, just beyond the fence that is rusted and sagging, its posts rotting from fungi and termites. Above the grove, three buzzards silently glide in narrowing circles. Suddenly one drops lower in the sky so that the tips of its wings nearly skim the top branches of the tallest tree, so that it's possible to discern the hideous features of its head.

Prey

In the dim yellow light the lamp gives off, he sits at the desk wearing nothing but a towel wrapped around his waist. The towel hangs open so that his entire left thigh and a glistening mass of black pubic hair are visible. The hair on his head is also wet. Water drops onto his shoulders hunched over the desk. He picks up a beer can, shakes it, puts it down. He picks up another and repeats the sequence. And again. This can is full. He raises it to his mouth and drinks until it's empty.

He holds a pen between his right thumb and index finger, drumming it against the blank pale green page of a notebook laid open on the desk. His eyes move up the wall to the ceiling where a spider is wrapping a moth in its web. His fingers stop drumming. He watches the spider spin fibers until there's nothing left of the moth but a tiny white obelisk suspended invisibly from the ceiling. The spider hangs motionless over the new corpse for a moment longer, then crawls up one thin fiber to the corner of the room, disappearing into a narrow crevice where the wall and ceiling meet.

His eyes move from the narrow crevice, down the single fiber to the tiny white obelisk. They linger there for a while, then crawl down the wall and across the desk until they reach the blank green page where the hand is just beginning to write across the top line in tiny uneven handwriting.

I desire

I want. I wish. I crave. I long for. I need.

Mosquito

From the bedroom there is the sound of rustling sheets, followed by a broken moan like unformed words. He stops writing and listens: now there's just the loud rhythmic chirping of a cricket marooned inside the house. Outside, the distant yapping of coyotes. He stands. The towel falls from his waist onto the floor. He starts to pick it up, changes his mind, goes to the bedroom and switches on the light.

Her eyes open, then close halfway against the glare of the ceiling bulb. She raises her head from the pillow and squints at him standing naked in the doorway.

"Damn it, Kale, why'd you turn on the goddamn light?"

"I wanted to wake you."

She groans and rolls onto her left side, away from the light.

He stands there a moment, staring at her spine shining with sweat. Finally, he turns off the light and goes to the bed and lays down next to her, his chest pressed tight against her back. His erection wedges itself into the crevice between her thighs.

"I'm tired, Kale."

"You're always tired."

"It's the weather. Heat makes me tired."

He doesn't move but stares at the back of her head, at her auburn hair clinging together in thick strands.

Snakes, he thinks. *Medusa.*

After a while he rolls away. He crosses his arms behind his head. Somewhere in the darkness he detects the shrill hum of a mosquito. The instant the humming stops, he feels a sting on the underside of his right arm. He doesn't move. He waits. Soon he feels another sting just above his ankle. He waits. Another sting. Another. . .

In the darkness he begins counting mosquitoes.

Dead calf

He makes his way through the cows and heifers and new calves, toward a narrow grove of trees at the pasture's north end. The underbrush is thick and green. He lifts his legs high over the bushes and vines and rotting logs. Directly ahead of him, in a small clearing bright with sunlight, a cow stands with her head bent over a small dark mound on the grass. He watches as she nudges the mound with her nose, then licks it roughly, her hind legs trembling. Her tail swings back and forth over the bloody placenta still hanging beneath it. He steps closer. The buzz and whine of flies is deafening.

The cow turns toward him and begins to bawl. She steps nearer the mound until her right front hoof presses against it. He continues moving toward her, talking softly, his boots becoming tangled every now and then in the mass of scrubs and low vines. When he's only a few feet away, he stops and squints. The cow bends down and again nudges the mound which doesn't move: its eyes, the color of watery milk, are rolled up inside its head.

Just before he sits on the fungal branch of a fallen tree and puts his head in his hands and closes his eyes, he sees the shadow of a bird pass over the corpse lying in the sunlit clearing.

Song

Who are we when we sing? Are we no different than who we are when we laugh or cry or scream? And if we're unchanged, if we remain precisely the same, then what good does singing do us?

Too bad

"What's the name of that song you're humming?"

"Don't know. Heard it on the radio this morning. Got a pretty tune, don't it?"

"Yeah. Willa sang it once. Down at the pond. She didn't know I was listening."

"That right?"

"I was putting up fence along the north creek and I heard this beautiful voice singing real loud. I walked up the hill and stood there in the cottonwood grove and saw her sitting on a felled tree beside the water. She had a stick in her hand. She was lifting the moss from the water with the stick and singing that song."

"That right?"

"When the song was over, she stopped singing. She just sat there with the stick in her hand, staring out over the pond. I waited almost a half-hour for her to start singing again, but she didn't. She just got up from the tree and threw the stick in the water and walked away."

"Too bad."

"I never knew she sang until then."

"This calf's got stomach worm, too."

Bankruptcy worm

"They're parasites, blood suckers, transmitted through manure. Among cattle they may cause poor weight gain and, in worst cases, anemia. Contagion is more prevalent during droughts, since cows must graze closer to the ground. Calves can be infected as soon as two weeks after birth. Because stomach worm can destroy profits from an entire herd, it's often referred to as *bankruptcy worm*."

*—Bill Buford's Bug Book
for Beginners, Volume 3*

Target practice

Hidden beneath an old towel on the floor next to the bed is a .22 long rifle loaded with hollow-point bullets.

A hollow-point bullet will enter and exit an empty aluminum can relatively cleanly, leaving little more than a dime-sized hole on either side. Conversely, as it enters flesh it will flatten upon impact and mushroom outward, causing a wound the size of a fist. Once inside the corpse-to-be, the lead may bounce around, rip through muscle and fat and gristle, deflect from bone or shatter it. Eventually the bullet will lodge. Or exit into air.

On still evenings just before the sun leaves the sky, before the dry wind rises from the valley, he hangs empty beer cans from the half-dead pine tree growing on the edge of the cliff that overlooks the valley and pond. With a spike nail he punches a hole in the top of each can, threads a piece of packing string down through the hole and up through the pour spout, then ties the string off. He drags an old wooden stepladder from the darkness of the unfinished basement, sets the ladder beneath the pine tree and ties ten or twenty beer cans to the lower branches. Then he goes into the bedroom and picks up the rifle and sits on the edge of the bed and shoots at the cans through the open bedroom window.

My turn

She flinches at the first rifle shot, her muscles contracting once and quickly. Usually she stops what she's doing and goes out and sits on the front porch and presses her hands over her ears and hums until the wind rises and it's too dark to see beer cans hanging from a tree. Other times she walks into the bedroom and says, "My turn."

Letter

Dear Richard,

How goes the living down South?

The dying in the Midwest is going fine. Our cistern went dry three weeks ago, so we had to start hauling water in from town. Kale cut the garden hose into tiny pieces last week. He says if he catches me wasting water on the marigolds again, he'll make salad out of them. Anyhow, it doesn't matter. The earth surrenders its moisture to the sky. The leaves of everything are curled up like fetuses.

This heat, this perpetual sunshine, it all makes me careless. For example, last night I knocked a jar of turpentine onto the floor and left it there. Just left it. The floor's wooden so now there's a stain on it like dried blood. Probably, Kale will shoot me when he sees it. And so what. As I said, it's a summer for death.

I'm lonely, big brother, and wish you'd come visit me. We could go for a walk in the timber and be found months later, dead of heat prostration.

With my love at least undying,
Willa

Precipice

"Willa!"

"What?"

"What the hell are you doing out there?"

"Waiting."

"Waiting for what?"

"For the wind."

"It's three in the morning. It's not going to rise."

"It always rises."

"We're in the middle of a drought. Come back to bed."

"I can't breathe, Kale."

"You're standing too close to the edge. Come on back inside."

"The wind always rises."

Wound

"I love you, Willa."

"Don't say that. It sounds false."

"Then what do you want me to say?"

"I don't know. Say you'd run back inside a burning building to get me."

"I would."

"But you'd do the same for your best cow, wouldn't you?"

"Probably."

"Then say you'd kill the cow for me. Say you'd shoot her between the eyes to keep me with you."

"Willa. . ."

She lifts his right arm and presses her lips to the soft-skinned underside near the hollow of his armpit. She sucks on the skin, then sinks her teeth into it until his eyes water, until he feels the puncture.

He grits his teeth. He swallows the scream.

Moon

There's a full moon. Always equitable, it dusts the far timbered hills and shrinking pond and dry valley. It illuminates the chalky whiteness of cliffs, the peeling clapboard house, the bleached gravel road. It enters through the open window and spreads itself over the bed like a sheet of fine gauze.

The bed: where two bodies are moving in slow syncopated choreography. Reflections of one another. Sky and water. Shoulder blades like vanishing wings of fallen angels. Breasts, buttocks, thighs catching the moonlight, bending it until it trembles in the darkness and heat and deafening windless silence.

She gasps. She does not exhale for what seems to him far too long. When the air finally spills out of her lungs, it exits as a howl which he opens his mouth to catch and bite into and make his own before pouring back inside of her.

He thinks: *this is what death resembles.*

Town

It's called Prosper, but it never really did. In 1891 it reached its peak population of 4,565. After that came a slow steady decline. Because it was not on the way to anywhere, no one passed through unless they were lost. Families went broke and moved on. Children grew up and moved away. Those who stay eventually die.

Prosper Cemetery contains 2,231 tombstones. The dead now outnumber the living by 1,372.

This, our life

"I'm going into town for a while. Want to go with me?"

"No."

"Why not?"

"There's nothing there."

"You never leave the farm, Willa."

"If I leave, it won't be for Prosper."

"What's that supposed to mean?"

"Jesus, Kale."

"What?"

"Doesn't it scare the piss out of you?"

"What?"

"This. Our life."

"What?"

"What. What. Christ. Go buy your goddamn beer."

Drowning in water

The town consists of a feed store, a grocer, a hardware store, a service station, one vet, one doctor, and a cafe that also sells liquor and romance novels. Farmers who've already plowed under their worthless crops now spend all day sitting in the cafe, eating white toast, drinking beer, and reading books with titles like *Dangerous Desire*.

They used to talk about the weather, but it never changes. Besides, one day Gil Rawlins shouted at them, "Don't wanna hear no more goddamn talk about this goddamn drought 'cause you cain't do nothin' 'bout it, hear? We're just a bunch of goddamn ants waitin' for God to come picnic-in'."

Next day Gil's wife walked into the cafe and stood there just inside the door, stone-faced, and announced that Gil had drowned himself in a pail of water. Dunked his head under and inhaled.

Therefore, also: they no longer talk about the weather out of respect for the dead.

Dust

Suppose it never rained again. Would the earth become so dry, so hard, we couldn't bury our dead? Or would it simply crumble? Turn to a fine yellow dust which, when blown by the wind, would bury our dead for us? Bury us, too?

Ashes to ashes.

Dust to dust.

Letter

Brother Richard,

For chrissake stop worrying about me so much. You've spent twenty some years worrying about me and it hasn't changed anything.

Anyhow, I'm not depressed. It's just this goddamn awful heat and no rain and bugs everywhere and calves and everything else dying.

Here it is: I'm pregnant. Goddamn *pregnant!* And Kale and me are just getting poorer every day. And you know what's worse? Maybe I'm going insane or maybe not, but it seems to me that Kale is turning into Dad right before my very eyes. He drinks an awful lot and he doesn't write anymore. He goes out to count the newest dead calves and then heads for town to drink, or for the canoe to fish, or for the bedroom to shoot beer cans in the pine tree. Sometimes I look at him and I see Dad, and then I look at myself and see Mom.

Okay, do worry about me. When do you get a vacation? Could you spare a couple of days for me? Please write. Our phone's been disconnected, a luxury we can no longer afford.

Very truly your loving and lonely sister,
Willa

Route

It's eighteen miles from the small white house to the small white town of Prosper. Four miles on bleached gravel roads, the rest on a winding blacktop.

He has driven this route so often he believes he could do it with his eyes closed, but he leaves them open. What he sees, however, is the woman laying naked beneath him, splayed, an erotic crucifix: arms wide, ankles crossed, toes pointed, head thrown back, mouth open, heart-scar inflamed. . .

His left hand steers the pickup. His right hand unzips his trousers and slips inside his briefs and grabs hold of his penis which is hard and damp with heat. He masturbates and drives. Eventually he weeps.

Writer

He studied Russian literature in college because, like Hemingway, he wanted to write better than Dostoyevski.

Now he concludes: *delusion and youth.*

He raises cattle, after all. The fact that he can recite whole pages from Chekhov and Tolstoy does not stop the ribs of cattle from showing, does not stop calves from dying, does not green the alfalfa, kill the stomach worm, make the woman want.

Then again, if he had not studied Russian literature, it's possible he wouldn't have met her. She enrolled in a *Fathers and Sons* graduate seminar by mistake. Thought it was a psychology course. He saw her panicked face that first day of class and fell in love with it. Chivalrous and lustful, he offered to tutor her. She refused him, said she'd have to suffer the consequences of her erroneous choice.

She flunked.

Cafe

It smells like bacon morning, noon and night. The walls are covered with thick yellow enamel paint and on top of that: fly specks, spatters of catsup, and a hardened film of grease.

There are two waitresses. The younger bleaches her brown hair blonde; the older dyes her grey hair black. They both have large wide breasts and wear lipstick that stays put for days.

The cafe is air conditioned but not enough. When the lunch hour is over, the waitresses sit behind the linoleum-topped counter with their legs spread apart, drying their crotches with the hot wind from a rotary fan. Farmers and ranchers come and go, sluggish and morose. They tip their caps and smile half-way.

He used to sit in a corner by himself, drinking tea, reading experimental fiction and scribbling in a spiral notebook with pale green pages. Now he sits at the counter, skimming through romance novels and drinking bad scotch chased with beer. When he holds his head a certain way—tilted to the left and downward—he can catch the excessive and profound scent of waitresses.

In the beginning. . .

. . . there was man and then there was woman and she said "I want you" and he assumed, "always."

Waitresses

The younger one watches sweat gathering above the man's lips, watches his nostrils flare each time the fan swings back around, filling her skirt with wind. She knows he has a woman at home—not a wife, though, so it doesn't really count.

She pulls open the neckline of her blouse, puckers up her lips and blows a deep breath scented with Juicy Fruit gum down into the tight valley between her breasts. She slips her right hand into her blouse and slowly slides her middle finger painted red up the white skin spotted with moles and sweat. Without turning her head she knows he's watching her. Though she is not a cruel person, cruelty sometimes rises up inside her like poisonous smoke: she lifts the hem of her skirt and takes the still wet middle finger of her right hand and runs it up the full length of her left thigh, pushes it toward her crotch and finally against her clitoris which she strokes once and gingerly, throwing her head back, moaning theatrically. She looks at him straight on.

His face flushes. He removes his eyeglasses. With deliberate concentration, he wipes the lenses on the hem of his shirt, rubs his eyes hard with the knuckles of his left hand and puts his glasses back on. He does not raise his eyes as he drops a five dollar bill on the counter and quickly, soundlessly, leaves.

The older waitress watches after him, then clucks her tongue. *Must be the heat,* she thinks. *The dryness, maybe. The resignation all around.*

Cloud

Above this particular brown ruined landscape, a cloud obscures the sun. It's a cumulonimbus: massive and gray, full of moisture. Eventually it spills itself.

Hot thermals spiral upward from the earth, burning up most of the rain long before it reaches the ground. Droplets succeeding in the long descent evaporate the moment they touch dirt or stone or plant or glass.

Rain. Like the illusion of rain.

God's little joke.

Ha ha.

The illusion of rain

A raindrop appears on the pickup's windshield. He first mistakes it for the juice of a colliding insect, then as the watery droppings of a sick bird.

A second drop appears. He slows down, takes his eyes from the road, studies the hot dusty windshield.

When the third and fourth drops strike, he pulls the pickup onto the shoulder of the blacktop and turns off the ignition. He holds his breath. He waits.

Baby

The odor of linseed oil and turpentine fills her nose, yet she's able to detect the scent of rain moving toward her. Although the sun shines outside the window, she can feel the slight coolness caused by the shadow caused by the cumulonimbus passing in front of the sun fifteen miles away.

The day they took her mother away it rained hard. The newest brood of ducklings scuttled out of the coal shed and threw back their heads and opened their beaks and drowned.

Something shifts inside her.

She thinks: *Baby? No. Just rain.*

Last breath

He opens the glove compartment and rummages through receipts and manuals and napkins and small hand tools until he finds an old pack of Camels. The cellophane is brittle: when he pulls out a cigarette, there's a crackling like rain on the dry leaves of cattails. He slides the cigarette beneath his nose and sniffs, then returns the pack to the glove compartment, hiding it beneath the papers and tools. He pops in the cigarette lighter and looks up at the sky.

The cloud passes without consequence.

Within recent memory, he sees the spindly black legs of calves collapsing, sees the bony spines folding, corpses dropping. He thinks their last breaths must resemble the sighs of women.

Feast

The far hills and dry valley and white chalky cliffs are spotted with shadows of buzzards circling the dead. They spin around and around in the air. They land. They feast. There is so much death they must vomit in order to take flight again.

Cicada

She sets the paintbrush on the edge of the wooden table and stands and goes to the front door and opens it and walks out onto the porch. She looks to the west where a massive gray-white cloud rides the horizon. There is no wind. The air hums, light bends.

As she walks down the front steps toward the low cliffs, her bare feet crush the dry empty skins of cicadas.

Cicadidae

"During July and August, adult cicadas crawl out of their nymph-stage 'skins' to feed and mate. You can find these brown, translucent shells hanging by the thousands on tree bark or shrubs, or scattered upon the ground."

—*Bill Buford's Bug Book for Beginners, Volume 2*

Blood

He watches a pair of cicadas mate on his windshield. The male extracts itself from the female and flies off. He stares at the female, watching her legs twitch on the hot windshield. Then he flips on the wipers.

Ten minutes pass. He pulls a bottle of scotch and a paperback titled *Tropical Heat* from behind the seat of the pickup. He stares at the book's cover, at the large high white perfectly round breasts of a woman swooning in the arms of a dark-skinned native. He opens the bottle and takes a long drink. The lighter pops out. He puts the cigarette between his lips, opens the book and begins reading. Even before reaching the end of the page, he's swollen tight with blood.

Tropical heat

Amanda feels the tropical heat of Manú's dark, throbbing sex bulging against her damp, fleshy thighs. Her heart pounds, her breath quickens, her breasts feel as if they will burst from her lacy décolletage. When at last he presses his hot, wet mouth over her full, crimson lips, plunging his tongue down her throat again and again, harder and harder, she loses all control and tears his loin cloth from his groin, clutching his taut, powerful buttocks, and panting, "Yes, Manú. . .Oh, yes! . . .Yes!"

—from the novel *Tropical Heat,*
by Veroniqué St. Charles

Lullaby

She removes her clothes and tosses them over the edge of the cliff. She pulls the comb from her chignon and lets her hair fall over her shoulders. White-skinned beneath a white sun, she presses her fingers over her belly just now beginning to swell, then moves to the sand pile and lets her naked body collapse onto it. Grains of quartz and mica and granite sear her skin. Tears well. She bites her bottom lip and tilts her head back and begins singing in a high shrill keening voice.

It's a lullaby without words. Her mother sang it to her once, before she spun herself to death.

By the time the cumulus travels fifteen miles to pass over the small white house and low cliffs and dry valley and vanishing pond and distant hills, she's asleep and there's no rain at all.

PART FOUR: SEPTEMBER

Radio

. . . Today's joke comes to us from Kenny Joe Rupard way the heck out in Prosper. Are y'all ready? Okay, question: What do you get when you cross a drought with a cornfield? Answer: Real drunk. . .

Sold

"Give you twenty-eight thousand for the whole lot of 'em."

"Twenty-eight?"

"I'm serious, now Kale. You ain't gonna get more than twenty in Taylorville. Wormy. No meat. Whole goddamn calf crop's nothin' but carrion."

"Twenty-eight sounds awfully low."

"Kale, I'm fond of you and Willa. Twenty-eight's generous."

"I don't know."

"It's a damn shame is what it is. Here. Have a drink on me."

"Thanks."

"Lord a'mighty! Goddamn flies havin' one helluva smorgasbord in this drought, ain't they?"

"Shit. Okay. Shit. Let's load 'em all up."

Sky

Before she wakes, she hears tires skidding on gravel and suddenly, briefly, dreams of snow.

He pulls into the driveway and slams to a halt at the top of the south road that leads into the valley. Yellow dust rises, mushrooms, hangs for a while in the air and then falls around him like bad twilight. He drinks whiskey and stares out past the dry brown valley and shallow pond and opposite hills that are mockingly green. He lifts his eyes higher, just above the horizon, and squints at the white sky which contains nothing but the low entropic circling of buzzards about to descend.

I want

I wish. I crave. I long for. I need. I desire.

Ache

She sits up in bed, her body heavy with water and fatigue, and crawls to the window and looks out to watch him drag the stepladder from the basement.

He hangs beer cans from the pine tree.

She lays her swollen breasts on the hot peeling paint of the sill. They ache.

Storm

There is no way to be certain that the storm building over the Rockies will not dissipate before it moves across the plains and into the heartland.

Meteorologists no longer make hopeful predictions.

The half-hearted religious no longer pray.

We have each other

"Where's the rifle, Willa?"
"You're drunk."
"Where'd you hide it?"
"You sold the herd, didn't you?"
"Give me the goddamn rifle!"
"We have nothing left, Kale."
"We have each other."
"Not even that."

Letter

Richard,
    I can't leave him. I've tried but I just can't.

Help me,
Willa

Rape

"We have each other."

"Get off me."

"I need you, Willa."

"Kale, get off me *now!*"

"I want to fuck you, Willa . . ."

"Jesus God, Kale!"

". . . fuck you . . ."

"Don't!"

". . . fuck . . ."

Praying mantis

On the gray trunk of a dead elm at the edge of a diminishing pond, a female mantis chews off the head of her courting male.

Mantis religiosa

"Because the transmission from the brain of a mantis to its body is so primitive and therefore slow, the headless body of the male will continue to dance around the female, slowly maneuvering into position directly behind her. Finally, it mounts and copulates."

—*Bill Buford's Bug Book*
for Beginners, Volume 8

Singing

He slides out of her, lifts himself up and stares down at the blood on her mouth and chin. He raises a finger to touch the wound on his cheek. It's deep: teeth marks form a perfect circle.

Her eyes are closed. She's breathing hard. Still, she dosen't weep.

He weeps. He says, "I'm sorry," over and over again. When his hand touches the small mound of her belly, she flinches but doesn't open her eyes.

Eventually he stands and pulls up his trousers and walks out of the house. As he starts down the road leading into the valley, he thinks he hears her singing a song he doesn't know.

360°

She walks from the bedroom to the kitchen to the open space to the living room and back to the bedroom. A perfect circle.

Heron

A canoe pushes through the thick moss covered with dead fish and flies and long thin white worms like bits of string. The stench is sickening. He lays his head against the hot aluminum and vomits into the water. His pores spill sweat and whiskey. His head aches. His eyes burn.

The sky is white, the sun is white.

A great blue heron watches him from the top of the dead elm. It lifts its wings and swoops down to the bank of the pond, then walks onto the cracked mud to peck at a dead fish. But it doesn't eat.

He waits for the bird to fill the silence.

Instead it struts back onto the dry clay bank and stands a moment longer, watching him. Finally, it arches its thin neck, flaps its oily wings, and ascends.

Target

She hums and loads the rifle with .22 hollow-point bullets.

There are twelve beer cans hanging from the branches of the pine tree. She starts on the right, one shot per can, and works her way toward the left. When she has hit the last can, she aims the scope three inches further, beyond the pine tree and low cliffs and dry valley. She sees his muscles rise with each downward swing of the oar, sees the sweat of his back, the brown of his neck, the black shining hair of his head. . .

Richard

The younger waitress gives him directions to the small white house eighteen miles on blacktop and bleached gravel roads. Halfway to the door he remembers to thank her, and turns, and sees her wetting her lips and arching her eyebrows. He says nothing.

He pulls into the driveway and parks the car in front of the house. He stares past the two misplaced oaks, at the peeling clapboard and lawn full of thistles, at the mound of dirty sand, the pine tree strung with beer cans. He frowns, sighs, gets out of the car and walks up the front steps littered with crushed cicada skins. He knocks and waits. Nothing. He opens the screen door, ducks his head inside and calls out: "Willa?" He puts his hands in and out of his pockets and jingles his change. Finally, he enters the house.

Although a cool wind is rising outside, inside it's hot. Flesh flies move from one room to another. The odor of turpentine and linseed oil causes his eyes to water. He calls out her name as he walks from the open space to the kitchen to the bedroom and into the living room, where he sees a wooden table covered with misshapen tubes of paint, sees a fragment of mirror resting precariously on the table's edge, sees an easel which he steps around in order to look at the painting of the woman, his sister, Willa: eyes set wide and bulging, hair rising like antennae, shoulders sprouting wings.

Before he has time to name the fear rising in his chest, a bright flash of light enters through the window behind him. He turns into it and sees:

Beyond the low white cliffs and dry brown valley, on a pond at the foot of the distant and miraculously green hills, a canoe spins slowly in the water. He steps up to the window and presses his forehead against the hot pane and squints.

He yells.

The moment he reaches the pond where the headless man is slumped in a canoe and the naked woman floats face-down among green moss and dead fish and flies and worms, the white sun vanishes behind what seems to be an endless bank of thunderheads.

It rains.

SAY WHAT YOU LIKE

1.

Some women are drawn to pain. Some men are drawn to the wounded. Who knows the reason or fault? Blame the father incapable of returning the daughter's persistent love. Blame the mother who loved the son too much, exchanging maternal affection for surreptitious fondling. Say what you like, it is more common than you think.

And the daughter who becomes a woman slumps through the world with the indictment *Unloved!* emblazoned on her forehead. And the son who becomes a man cloaks his anger in the same sweet innocence that brought his mother to her knees. And the woman seeks out just such a man. And the man seeks out just such a woman. Eventually they find each other.

2.

A park in autumn. The sky a frightening blue, thick and crystalline, as in the repetitive nightmares of a fever. The earth upon which the new lovers throw themselves smells of dying, but they do not notice.

He tells her stories from his childhood wherein his naiveté proves him both the hero and the buffoon. Her stories, though begun in humor, always end in loss. Because they do not know each other well, they believe it's love into which they're falling, not darkness.

3.

Q: *Define relationship.*

A: *A man and a woman relating to each other.*

Q: *On what level?*

A: *It doesn't matter. The level is the adjective. Platonic relationship. Intimate relationship. Oedipal relationship. Unhealthy, stormy, bent relationship.*

4.

They talk on the telephone every day. Their conversations last for hours. Until the skin over the gristle of her ear becomes inflamed. Until the mouthpiece of his receiver is slippery with respiration. They cover topics as diverse as politics, religion, unemployment, racism, ecology, the weather. . . . Yet not once do they say, "Define relationship. Specifically, ours."

Why should they? Although they silently question it every day, neither has yet arrived at a satisfactory answer.

5.

He has a dog. She has a cat.

His dog needs him, depends on him. When he leaves town for more than a day, the dog doesn't eat, doesn't sleep, just lays on his bed morning, noon and night. Sighing.

Her cat ignores her until it's ready to be caressed. If she picks it up too soon, it sinks its claws into her arms, and wriggles and twists and scratches until she sets it free. When she comes home from a long absence, it lifts its head, blinks, goes back to its nap.

He loves his dog. She loves her cat. Easy: they're animals.

6.

Oh, and then there's sex. That event where two people who have nothing in common find something in common.

"Do you like it when I do this?"

"No. It hurts."

"It hurts?"

"Yes."

"When I do this?"

"Yes!"

"Does it hurt too much?"

"How much is too much?"

"That's what I want to know."

"That's what I want to know, too."

7.

The sky holds back for months. Finally, it snows.

They find themselves on a high embankment overlooking a deep drift. He leaps into it, landing first on his feet, then on his hands. He turns to her, laughing, and says, "Jump!"

She shakes her head no.

He says, "Jump!"

She says, "I'm afraid."

He says, "Jump! I'll catch you!"

She steps to the edge of the embankment.

On the street, someone he knows drives by and honks. He turns and waves, just as she leaps into air.

8.

He dreams of his mother:

She comes to him in the night, her breasts settling around his head, her fingers curling around his cock. He moans and begins to suckle her. Her grip grows tighter as he swells toward a wet dream. Suddenly the tone shifts. His mother's breasts are huge. Their slick weight heaves against his mouth, nose, eyes. He can't breathe. His moans become whimpers as he struggles beneath her and against his uncontrollable erection. Desperate, he strikes out wildly, blindly, his fists landing on the face of the woman sleeping beside him.

She screams awake, waking him too. "For godsake, look what you've done! My nose is bleeding!"

He touches her shoulder with one finger. "I'm sorry. I had a nightmare."

He throws off the blankets and looks down between his legs. "Jesus."—he is more surprised than chagrined—"I've pissed all over myself."

9.

Q: *When did the violence begin?*

A: *Don't be ridiculous, it's always been there. Think back: that afternoon at the farmer's market when he held out a plump round tomato polished to a ruby shine, and she said, "Oh, it's perfect! That's the one!" And he looked at her, and grinned, and squeezed the tomato in his fist until it exploded. There were seeds everywhere.*

10.

Occasionally he hits her.

11.

In a resturant, she stabs a tomato wedge and offers it to him across the table.

He leans forward, opens his mouth wide and folds his lips around the pink flesh. He sucks it from the fork.

She watches him chew.

He swallows.

He says, "Thanks."

She stares at a tomato seed stuck to his chin and says, "You're welcome." The seed remains on his chin throughout the rest of the meal.

12.

Angels provide moments of perfect wisdom. It's their job. And, being angels, they know the exact proportion of enlightenment allotted each soul in order to keep a distinction between God and Man, between Man and Satan.

These moments are brief and do not come often. But when they arrive, one should not discount them. Or watch them vanish in the smoke of the heart, damaged and stupid. Or let them drown in the wetness of desire.

13.

She opens her eyes in the hollow darkness to witness his clenched teeth, his furious brow. For a moment she forgets that he's inside her and thinks: *I've been here before, the blind guest of hatred.*

He quickly turns his head away, buries it in the damp curls along her neck, and moans.

Believing she has pleased more than his libido, she releases the lucid thought, her one angelic allotment. What a mistake.

14.

He takes the wrong exit.

She tells him so.

He says, "Shut up."

She does.

But her silence is not enough. He pushes the car over the speed limit. She tells him to slow down. He speeds up. A sharp curve comes into view. She pleads with him. He grins. When they enter the turn, she grabs hold of the dashboard and starts to cry. Tires squeal. She is thrown against the door as the left side of the car rises from the pavement. He uses the steering wheel to balance himself while easing up on the accelerator. There is a fraction of a second when he is not exactly certain he can bring the car under control, when she is exactly certain she will die.

The moment passes. The road is straight.

15.

She will never ask herself: *Why didn't I leave then, the first time he made me cry?*

He will never ask himself: *Why did I feel such pleasure upon witnessing her first tear?*

16.

A headboard made of oak. The man and woman making love.

He's on his knees and inside her. Her calves are squeezed tight around his neck, her feet locked behind his head. He slides his hands under her bottom and repeatedly dips himself into her cervix, thrusting her body nearer the headboard.

The inevitable sound of her skull hitting the oak excites him. She is excited by his excitement. She starts to come. He thrusts harder. He starts to come. She comes. He comes. They climax simultaneously, vanishing into their respective absence. This has never happened before.

It will never happen again, but they will keep trying. From now on sex will be followed by a cigarette for him, an aspirin for her.

17.

She loves him too much and fears he does not love her enough.

He does not love her enough and fears she loves him too much.

18.

Occasionally he hits her. Not in the face, never in the face.

19.

He looks at his reflection in the mirror. "I'm handsome, aren't I?"

She looks over his shoulder into the mirror. "Yes." She looks at her face. "I'm not as handsome as you, but I'm beautiful in my own fashion."

He shrugs, grins a Hollywood smile, taps a fingernail on a white front tooth, then sobers. "Someday I'll be an old man, with gray hair and a wrinkled dick."

"That will never happen."

"What, that my hair will never turn gray, or my dick will never be wrinkled?"

She turns to leave. A smile twitches at a corner of her mouth. "You'll never live to be an old man."

20.

He drinks too much. Every occasion is an occasion for drowning.

His father died of cirrhosis at the age of 52. Sometimes he dreams of his liver swelling to the size of a holiday turkey, of his mother slicing him open, removing the liver and eating it with a spoon. These are the nights he wakes up sweating, saliva pouring onto his tongue from all sides, a nausea inside as if something foul and noxious had ruptured.

She wakes to the sound of him vomiting. When he climbs back into bed, she pretends to be asleep, to have heard nothing.

21.

A dark night like spilled ink.

He trembles without knowing why. She presses herself against him to stop the trembling.

"What do you dream about?" he asks.

"Nothing," she replies, "I don't dream."

"Everyone dreams."

"Not me."

"Then why do you cry in your sleep?"

"Do I cry in my sleep?"

"Like a dog. Like a whimpering dog."

"I'm not a dog."

"You whimper. You must be dreaming. Your dreams must be nightmares."

"That's probably why I forget them before I wake up."

"How do you do that?" he asks. (She is surprised by his sincerity.) "How do you forget your dreams?"

22.

It does not occur to him that his anger is permanent: a worm, a larva, a grub that every now and then wriggles and twists and chews on his insides until he thinks he will explode. Which he does: rage cloaked in boyishness, in adolescent flirting, in a thing difficult to name *rage*.

23.

There is no such thing as a short winter. It can snow or not snow, sleet or not sleet, freeze or be mild, but people will always say, "What a long winter!"

It's the lack of sunlight. Gray days and disproportionate darkness. Flesh going pale and soft on couches and in beds. Rooms closing in. A sense of inhaling for the last time.

24.

They wake one winter morning and do not bother to get up. They make love, read books, take naps, eat, whine about their lives, the weather, politics. . .

By nightfall, the sensation of skin against skin irritates her like hives. She rolls over, away from him, and drops an arm over the side of the bed. She stares out the window. The moon momentarily breaks through the low gray clouds and sends a tender ray through the blinds into her eyes. Slowly, like a sigh for the deaf, she reaches toward the light.

25.

He's convinced that the reason he cannot love her is that he has never recovered from his first love. Or was it his third? In any event, he has not recovered and therefore cannot love this woman who loves him with such magnified desperation that he sometimes finds himself sitting with his head out the bathroom window in the middle of the night—temperature below zero—just to make certain he's still breathing.

26.

Sometimes just before waking she hears a voice—her mother's perhaps—whisper: *Leave! Leave now! While there's less pain in going!*

27.

At some point in pre-history a two-legged creature migrated from a warm climate to a cold climate and survived the transition. It's called acclimation.

Question: *Why didn't the creature leave the harsh environment?*

Hypothesis: *Change is more stressful than a stressful routine.*

28.

After ten months a woman knows her relationship with a man is the emotional equivalent of a gulag.

After ten months a man knows his relationship with a woman gives him bad dreams and not infrequently diarrhea.

Yet they stay together. And stay and stay and stay. . . Why?

It's better than being alone, she thinks.

It's better than being alone, he thinks.

Hypothesis: *No. It's not.*

29.

Occasionally he hits her. Not in the face, never in the face. To hit her in the face would make his anger obvious and he would be reminded of his anger for a period far longer than the duration of his momentary rage. He hits her on the arm, the ribcage, the thigh. He slaps her ass, pinches her nipples, bites her tongue. He hisses, "I'm going to fuck your brains out," and then makes an attempt.

She allows it. Later, she stands naked before him and touches a circle of blue on her shoulder and pulls down her lower lip in a pout and says, "Look. Look what you did to me."

And he looks at the bruise and gingerly presses a finger to it until she winces, and he says, "Oh, my poor baby, I'm sorry." He kisses the wound. "I am so very sorry."

Still pouting, she nods her forgiveness.

30.

The first crocus bends upward through the snow, toward the suggestion of light.

31.

She hits him with words because she can curl them tighter than fists.

I'm going to go back to school," he tells her over breakfast. "I'm going to go back and get my MBA."

"You won't," she tells him.

He looks at her.

"You're too fucking lazy. You have no motivation, no ambition. You will never, never go back to school."

He looks at her a long while. Finally, he splits open the yolk of an egg and watches it spill over his plate.

32.

Turnstiles move in one direction only. Once a person passes through there's no turning back. And that person will spend an irretrievable chunk of a lifetime wandering through a mistake. Weeping, obsessing, stumbling over words and gestures. Simply because the fare was non-refundable.

Turnstiles also exit.

But these are emotional capitalists we're talking about, born and bred. They're compelled to get their money's worth. Their heart's worth. Even if it's pain they're buying.

33.

Give him what he wants, she thinks, *so he'll stay.*

Don't give her what she wants, he thinks, *so she'll keep coming back.*

34.

He rakes wet leaves left over from the previous autumn. She reads a magazine while the sun burns her shoulders. Trees shudder and hiss in the wind. A blue jay lands on a lilac bush and screams.

She looks up from her magazine, looks at the blue jay, looks at the man raking leaves. She calls out, "Do you love me?"

He stops raking and turns. "What?"

"Do you love me?"

He leans on the rake and looks up at the sun. He wipes his sweating face with the sleeve of his tee-shirt. He looks at her. "No."

She nods, stands, lays down the magazine and goes into the house. She strolls from one room to the next, gathering up her things: a toothbrush, earrings, a sweater, socks, purse, car keys. She walks out.

35.

There can be no happy ending.

Couples become bored, fall out of love, grow apart, hate, leave one another for someone else or for solitude. Or stay together until one-half of the couple dies, leaving behind something not quite complete: a goat with its hind legs missing.

36.

He runs to the front yard in time to see her car disappearing down the street. He stretches out his hand and imagines a wooden arc tossed into the air.

"Boomerang," he says.

He closes his eyes, curls his fingers around the imaginary wood, and grins: "Boomerang."

37.

If there can be no happy ending, then what ending do you want?

Okay, fine. Let's say she leaves him one day and does not come back. Ever. He will wait for her to return. When she does not, he will be surprised, then will forget his surprise, and enjoy the sudden freedom of his solitude. She will wait for him to ask her to return. When he does not, she will hope he will never ask, then will forget about him asking or not asking, and enjoy the sudden freedom of her solitude.

Every now and then something—a melody, a particular breeze, a scent—will cause them to remember. But these memories will stir nothing inside, will trigger no chemical reaction, no palpitations, no trembling, no nausea, no remorse. Just memory: there and then not there. Like walking through a cloud of cigar smoke.

38.

Q: *Who are these people?*

A: *Perhaps the woman is me. Perhaps the man is you. Say what you like, we're all fallible. If it's not this fault, it's that one. Invariably: I hate your faults, you hate mine. We barely tolerate our own. More often we deny their existence. Still we're pulled together, sadly, by an intangible thing whose presence we loathe and absence we mourn.*

"Love," she says (I say).

"Love," he says (you say), "or a close imitation of it."

39.

There will be a day in autumn when the sky above a park is a frightening blue, thick and crystalline, as in the repetitious nightmares of a fever. Everywhere will be the smell of dying: pungent, vaguely familiar.

Neither the man nor the woman will witness the blueness, catch the scent of death, feel the dampness ease into their bones. And although they will not be present to glimpse the brief shadow cast upon them, geese will fly south anyway.